D1795216

A
SOUTH
CENTRAL
Love Story

Ayodele Olaniyan

authorHOUSE®

AuthorHouse™ UK
1663 Liberty Drive
Bloomington, IN 47403 USA
www.authorhouse.co.uk
Phone: 0800.197.4150

© 2019 Ayodele Olaniyan. All rights reserved.

No part of this book may be reproduced, stored in a retrieval system, or
transmitted by any means without the written permission of the author.

Published by AuthorHouse 04/16/2019

ISBN: 978-1-7283-8741-3 (sc)
ISBN: 978-1-7283-8740-6 (e)

Print information available on the last page.

Any people depicted in stock imagery provided by Getty Images are models,
and such images are being used for illustrative purposes only.
Certain stock imagery © Getty Images.

This book is printed on acid-free paper.

Because of the dynamic nature of the Internet, any web addresses or
links contained in this book may have changed since publication and
may no longer be valid. The views expressed in this work are solely those
of the author and do not necessarily reflect the views of the publisher,
and the publisher hereby disclaims any responsibility for them.

Contents

Acknowledgments

I just want to say thank you to a few people who kept me going through this project. They have been a constant help in pushing me to finish while keeping me excited about it.

I want to say thank you to God; if it wasn't for His strength and power, I would never have had the idea let alone started and finished this project.

I'd also like to thank my family and friends for their support. Dad, Mum, and siblings, thank you so much for your support. Wisdom, Dean, Kevin, Lanre, Amadu, Faith Rejoice, and Eunice—I want to say thank you to you all. And Apostle ATB Williams, thank you for being an inspiration for me also.

Prologue

Moving to Los Angeles, California, Cordell and his mother expected to start a new life, again. As they drove into Los Angeles, they saw the sunshine and saw the beautiful scenery. Being here made Cordell extremely excited. He thought of Hollywood, being around stars and ballplayers. Little did he know his mum would drive past it all to end up in the projects. In particular, they were going to South Central, Los Angeles, around the corner from Crenshaw.

Looking around as he came closer to home, he started to see homes that resembled those from his past lives in Baltimore, New York, and Washington. There were boarded abandoned homes, dried blood on the street, a liquor store on every corner, and a few gun stores nearly every four blocks.

He looked at his mother, and his mother looked at him. "Mum, this is no different from Baltimore."

"Cordell, I know it doesn't look good, but the house itself it so beautiful inside. The previous owner did it up and is renting it to us."

"Yeah, but Mum, I'm still going to be around the same type of dudes I was around in Baltimore."

"Well, you've done well to stay away from that street

en after your brother died in it, so I'm sure you can ....inue to focus on school and going to UCLA."

Cordell's past was definitely not a great one. Growing up in Baltimore hadn't been easy. His brother had been a drug dealer and run his own crew and committed countless murders. Cordell saw poverty, crime, and sex way too early due to his environment. His brother made it very clear that he should avoid that life and focus on school and sports. Cordell focused on school and basketball. He was a model student and a talented basketball player, but he preferred education to basketball. Later in his life, when his brother was murdered, his mother asked to move to the LA branch for her work. Working for a countrywide private healthcare general practice gave her the ability to relocate as a nurse. The manager she previously had in Baltimore understood the fragile nature of her loss. Cordell's mother was extremely good at her job and therefore the company wanted to keep her and knew she'd be an asset. The switch over would be easy and quick. Luckily the new manager in LA had an opening lead nurse role and was happy to accept her. She had a good manager in Baltimore and hoped the new manager in LA would be just as lovely.

Pulling up to the new house, Cordell and his mother got out, and Cordell looked around. He saw Blood (Piru) gang members at the end of his street watching him. He thought, *I guess we'll see whether I can avoid it this time.*

1

"Cordell?" An assuring tone cried out through the stillness of the early morning in the neighborhood.

"Yes, Ma?"

"Be careful, honey. Have a good day," she replied with a warm smile and a wave.

Walking off, Cordell felt ready to start a new life in Los Angeles, South Central. Cordell and his mother had moved around a lot over the years due to her work, but this time, it was different; she said they'd be staying in LA for good. Before LA, Cordell and his family had moved from Washington to New York to Baltimore before reaching their final destination of LA. Baltimore was where they had stayed the longest. He spent most of his teenage years— ages twelve to seventeen—in Baltimore. Baltimore made him. The gritty streets of his neighborhood made him street-smart.

Los Angeles was different from Baltimore. For a start, the weather was sunny, and it was always warm. The streets were a little cleaner, and the females in LA were a lot more attractive. Fashion and the way people dressed seemed a little different too.

Though LA was completely different from Baltimore, a hood was a hood, and the projects were the projects. He could somehow completely translate Baltimore to LA. As he walked into the entrance courtyard, he studied his environment, locating the basketball court, water fountains, back entrances, and all the buildings. The buildings were different. Some seemed modern and some seemed a little older and under refurbishments but some parts of the buildings were still accessible to the students for lessons. Different subject departments were put in these different school buildings within the school campus. He sat on a bench in the middle of the courtyard facing the entrance to take in his new environment.

Sitting on the bench, Cordell studied his school schedule to assess where he needed to put extra time into studying. He had just turned eighteen and transferred from a Baltimore high school to Crenshaw High School in LA. Cordell's grades had transferred from his previous school to Crenshaw High without any problems. He would not have to retake any classes, as he had a high grade point average. Getting into UCLA was going to be achievable.

While he sat on the bench, two boys named Jayden and Marcel approached him in a friendly manner as they analyzed him. "What's up, nigga? You the new kid, right?" Jayden asked.

Cordell studied them in a manner that resembled a nomad lion looking to protect himself from a coalition of pride males. Cordell knew he could not get this wrong. He was fully aware of the repercussions that could potentially have. "Yeah, dawg, I'm Cordell."

"So what's up, nigga? You a Crip or a Blood?" asked Marcel.

Cordell studied their body language and assessed the colors of their clothing to make sure he didn't say anything that would bring him direct enemies on the first day. He looked them up and down and tried to see if they had any bandanas hanging out of their jeans. "Nah, homie. I'm neither. I don't do that gangbanging stuff." He made sure to approach his response with careful consideration and, therefore, produced a countenance that seemed innocent and unlearned of that particular issue.

"Aight, cool. You're better off hanging around us so you know who to avoid, my nigga," said Jayden.

A sigh of relief came from Cordell, and a shake of his head emphasized he was grateful to not have an encounter with gangbangers straight off the bat. He stood up and joined the two boys as they walked toward the main building of the school where all the home-room classes were. The room had big windows which let in the lighting from the outside. Considering that the sun accompanied with clear blue skies, was usually the normal weather in LA – schools including Crenshaw High School saved a lot of money on the light bills.

"What home-set you in?" asked Marcel.

Checking his schedule, Cordell replied, "Miss Clawdell."

"Oh, that's with us," stated Marcel.

Walking through the school, Cordell noticed that everyone knew Marcel and Jayden. Through the halls, everyone greeted him. They even greeted Cordell because he was with them.

Jayden, Cordell, and Marcel sat in the middle of their homeroom, contributing to the chitchat of the room. Soon, Ava Phillips came into the classroom, smiling at her friend's joke as they walked to their seats at the front of the class. She never noticed Cordell, but he was struck by her beauty. A Kelly Rowland type, she had a smooth, rich, sepia-like skin color. She possessed hazel eyes and a face that looked as if you might cut it out of a fashion magazine. Ava had long legs, a flat stomach, a small waist, wide hips, a taut backside, and small feet. Standing at five feet nine inches with a sweet smile and deep dimples, she could not go unnoticed. She had a long weave in, side-parted and put in a ponytail that accentuated her facial features.

"Homie, who is that?" Cordell asked Marcel and Jayden, interested in getting to know her.

"Who, her?" Marcel asked as he pointed at Ava.

"Yeah, her, man."

"She fine, right, homie? All the dudes in this school think that too. She's Ava," Jayden stated.

"OK, calm down, students, calm down," said Miss Clawdell, their home-room teacher, to start the class. "We have a new student here in the classroom. Cordell, can you come and tell the room about yourself, please?"

As the teacher asked Cordell this, the whole class turned to face him. As Ava turned, her eyes met Cordell's eyes, and his good looks took her aback. Cordell stood at six feet two inches. He had a deep, cool brown skin tone, similar in color to the sand in the Sahara Desert. His facial bone structure was warm and perfectly symmetrical, and he had light brown eyes. He had a fade haircut, and his full beard looked silky smooth. With his broad shoulders and athletic build, Cordell worked out hard, all right. Ava smiled a little as their eyes met.

"Hi, everyone," Cordell said at the front of the classroom. "I was born in Washington and moved to Baltimore, and then recently to LA. I love basketball and reading. Thanks." As he sat back down, he gave a little smile to Ava, and she gave him a look he took to mean, *I'm not that easy, nigga.*

Homeroom was a breath of fresh air for Cordell. The teacher instructed the students to move the desks to the back of the room and form a circle in the middle of the room with their seats. Cordell sat between Jayden and Marcel and analyzed everyone in the classroom. When he got to analyzing Ava, he turned his head to one side and then to the other. He thought, *She has to be mine. I give it six months.* Then he smiled.

"So, class, today we are going to talk about our future endeavors and learn from each other," stated the teacher. "Where should we start? *Hmm*, Ava, what are you planning to do after high school?"

"Well, miss, I'm going to UCLA to study fashion and magazine journalism. I want to be a fashion writer and become editor in chief for *Elle* magazine," she replied with a smile and a look over to Cordell.

"That is amazing, Ava. OK, let's see. Where should we go next? Cordell, it's your turn. What's next for you?" Having heard his name called out, he looked at the teacher and pointed to himself. "Yes, you, Cordell," she replied, smiling.

"OK. Well, I am going to UCLA too, and I'm studying sports broadcasting and creative writing. I want to be a sports anchor for ESPN and the NBA, as well as a multiple-time best-selling author." He addressed the group while looking at Ava.

Ava thought, *Finally, a dude with ambition. Where has he been all this time?*

"We have some ambitious young men and women. Jayden, you go."

"Well, miss, I'ma G, right? So I'm gonna have all the honeys in the hood," Jayden responded jokingly. Miss Clawdell looked at him with a very confused expression to show her disdain for that confession. "I'm joking, miss. I'm also going to UCLA to study business and economics." Marcel said he was also going to UCLA, to play college basketball and study sports journalism. Marcel was one of the top college basketball prospects in the country.

The teacher continued going around the whole room. Not only were young black individuals ambitious, they also knew there was a life beyond the neighborhood and gang violence. They realized that just because they were in the hood, it didn't mean they could not grow.

After the first three lessons of the day, there was a thirty-minute break. Cordell, Jayden, and Marcel played a game of HORSE on the basketball court. "So, Cordell, what's the streets like in Baltimore?" Marcel asked as he was just about to shoot the ball.

"Well, it's definitely different from LA. We don't have the gangbanging culture. We just have drug dealers. So everyone is straight until someone becomes too greedy, which happens all the time. So a drug dealer and his crew may rob another drug dealer, and that starts a war. A lot of shootings happen, man."

"You got any siblings, C?" asked Jayden.

"Y'all calling me C now? Well, I did have an older brother, but he's dead now," answered Cordell, looking straight into Jayden's eyes and creating an awkward atmosphere.

"How'd he die?" asked Jayden in order to quickly fill the silence.

"He was doing a drug run, going to a special client's house. And when he got there, he saw the drug dealer he robbed and tried to run. But as he turned around, the nigga's crew was there, and they shot him there in the girl's house. She set him up." There was silence for around five seconds after Cordell finished. His head dropped in the silence. "Anyway, what's up with Ava? Is she single?" he asked in order to get away from the awkward sadness he felt when speaking about his brother's death.

"Ava? Nah, C, she's single, but she has a crazy ex-boyfriend," Marcel replied.

"If you were a smart nigga, you would stay away from Ava, man. Her ex-boyfriend is a Blood," Jayden added in a sympathetic tone as if to warn him that as much as he liked her, Cordell couldn't go there because she had a possessive ex.

The South Central neighborhood in which Cordell, Jayden, Marcel, and Ava lived was infested with Blood gang members. This neighborhood had no direct rivals, as Crip gang members were not located really close to them, although many Crip members were enrolled at Crenshaw High School. "Foreal, she was with a gangbanger? But she seems different, though—like, what attracted her to him?" replied Cordell.

"I wish I could tell you, but I don't know. I ain't got all the answers!" Jayden exclaimed.

2

School eventually ended, and Cordell went home. He placed his bag on the seat he allocated as the place where he would always find his school bag. He had everything in a certain place. *Neat* was an understatement for Cordell. His room looked as if nobody ever slept there, as if he always kept it tidy and in prime condition for an unsuspecting family member to spring up and decide to stay over without consultation.

3

Friday—it has finally come, yes! Friday, Cordell thought after school one week. It had been three months since the initial move and he was beginning to feel a little more confident in his surroundings. He started dressing and behaving more like the LA folk and was beginning to add more friends. In the evening, there was always a street party in downtown Crenshaw on Friday. All the cool cats and gangbangers and pretty girls were there. Jayden and Marcel always went. Cordell only went occasionally, but today was one of those occasional days.

Going home, Cordell glowed with a beaming smile because he could go to the Crenshaw street party today since he had done all his schoolwork early. He neatly put his school bag back where he kept it and had a shower.

As he got ready listening to a '90s R&B playlist, his mother caught him dancing. "Cordell, make sure you look after yourself, OK? And don't be later than midnight, OK?"

The party started at 7:30 p.m., so he was happy with the curfew his mother set. "Yes, Ma, I'll be back before midnight." Looking good, Cordell smiled in the mirror and thought, *Ava can't resist me looking like this. She's gonna want all of this!* He laughed and went downstairs to see Jayden and Marcel waiting.

"G, you ready?" Marcel asked.

"Homie, I'm ready."

Arriving on the scene at the downtown party, walking through the strip on Crenshaw Avenue off Slauson Street where the massive outside car park was - Marcel, Cordell, and Jayden greeted as many people as they could see. Cordell had lived in the neighborhood for a while now and was building friendships within the area. The boys found their core group and started hanging just as the rest of the young people on the strip were. "Do you niggas believe in God?" Darnell asked inquisitively.

"Yeah, nigga, of course I do. How else would we be here, because I ain't no monkey, homie," answered Cordell.

"You think God is a woman?" Marcel asked.

"Nah, but why does that matter? He's just in charge, nigga," replied Jayden.

Ava stood at the counter of a Slurpee cart, receiving her drink. Cordell arrived behind her and said, "What's up, gorgeous? You enjoying yourself over here?"

"Hey, Cordell. Yeah, it's good, but someone has taken awhile to come over and talk to me."

"I was waiting to get you alone," he replied, showing a cheeky but sweet little grin.

She couldn't resist, and she smiled with an expression of shyness. "Well, next time, just come over and say hi. I'm always with them, my girls don't bite so one moment can't hurt."

"Let me have some of that drink."

"Nigga, no … OK, you can have a little." Taking the drink, Cordell had one sip, another sip, and then another. By the time he gave the drink back to her, he had nearly finished it. "You finished my drink!" Ava exclaimed with a smile. Cordell smiled and walked off; his charm had worked for him. Ava thought, *He is so cute; I can't be mad at him. I need to slow down.*

"Eh, homie, what were you saying to Ava? You had her smiling and giggling. Let a nigga know so I can do it with that fine girl right there," Jayden stated.

"Jay, it's a gift; you can't teach that, nigga," Cordell replied.

As all this unfolded, Ava's ex was watching and paying close attention to Cordell. Trouble was brewing for him and Ava.

4

Kenan was Ava's ex. He was a gangbanging young man willing to do anything to get her back, or at least keep guys away from her. Kenan loved the attention he got from her, being that he forced that attention. But he just loved attention in general. His need for approval and attention came from the disappointment his dad caused him, as he had constantly moved in and out of Kenan's life from a young age, and his mother's constantly working. The issue was Kenan didn't know that was the cause of the void he felt. Not understanding that made Kenan seek approval in the older gangbangers who showed him attention, which he viewed as love. Ava's issue with Kenan was not so much the gangbanging, as it was part and parcel of their world, but his controlling nature.

Kenan walked up to Ava with a serious demeanor and asked her, "Who was that nigga that made you laugh so much? Why you talking to that nigga? Are you trying to embarrass me?"

Ava looked him up and down, then focused on his face. With a dirty look and a disgusted tone, she replied, "Excuse me. Who on earth do you think you are talking to? You do not own me, nor are we together anymore, so all your questions are irrelevant, and I'm done with this conversation." She walked off and met with her friends without giving a look back.

Kenan had never ever been spoken to like that by a female; he was used to females doing whatever he wanted. Ava and Cordell may have won this round, but he would make it very hard for them from that moment on.

5

Kenan was an angry young man, but he could not pinpoint why he felt like that. He understood he never had a father figure in the home, but he had them on the streets, so he never felt he had daddy issues. When he was growing up, his mother had to work two jobs in order to feed Kenan; therefore, he had a lot of time to himself, and he used it for his pleasure.

His mother worked at her first job from 8:30 a.m. to 5:00 p.m. and at her second job from 7:30 p.m. to 3:30 a.m. Kenan spent his time during her working hours messing around at school and then hanging around the 185 Bloods from the age of eight. He was honed and groomed in the culture of the streets; he held a gun for the first time at the age of nine and owned his own gun at twelve. From hanging around them and learning from them, he was initiated into the 185 Bloods crew at fourteen.

Kenan's mother was never around to see the change in him. He always felt like his mother hated him because she didn't see him throw his first touchdown or learn how to ride a bike. Kenan thought, *Why would you have a child if you were never there for them?* and therefore invested his hope in his elders on the street. The intensity in his eyes and in his attitude to learn from them was incredible; he went to school to learn how to make more money on the streets, which paved the way for him to inherit the crew.

At nineteen, he was leading the crew and led it with such wisdom that those older than him in the crew diligently watched him to learn. Knowing how smart he was, he knew he could go to college and succeed, but he thought that it was better to be the man on the streets. Kenan was handsome, charming, intelligent, charismatic, and meticulous—he never left a stone unturned and was quiet. All those who underestimated him because of those virtues soon realized how violent, vicious, and aggressive he was.

On a hot Thursday afternoon, Kenan sat in the passenger seat of a Jeep on the block talking to some of his boys who sold cocaine for him, just giving them instructions and telling them how to be careful of an undercover cop, when a young man from another block walked past, popped his chain, and ran. Kenan's boys chased him. He dropped, and they caught him; they beat him up before taking him to Kenan.

Kenan stepped out of the Jeep and charmingly said in a soft and inviting tone, "What'up, G? You a brave nigga, ain't you? You know, you shouldn't be 'round here, nigga. You from Long Beach; I bet you never thought I knew, huh? But it's OK. You live and you learn, right?" Putting his arm around the young man's shoulder, Kenan went on to say, "I'll drop you home, but first, let me check if you got a weapon on you. No weapons in my ride—that's the rule."

After searching him and finding nothing, Kenan opened the car door for him and closed it after he sat comfortably. Kenan then smiled at him and got into the car. The driver locked the car door and drove off. Kenan's right-hand man, Angel, sat at the back with the young man. As they were driving, the young man realized that the men were taking him not home but to an abandoned house. They took him out of the car and sat him on a solitary chair in a room and tied him up.

After leaving him alone in that house for a few hours, they returned with pit bulls that looked as if they only ate human flesh. Kenan let loose the three pit bulls, and they attacked the boy, ripping him to pieces. Kenan watched the whole event happen as if he were learning a lesson from his previous street teachers, not batting an eyelid. The boy died a couple of hours later of his horrific wounds, and Kenan dumped him back in his neighborhood, where he should have been.

Looking at Kenan, someone would have thought he was a sports star or a musician because he was a very handsome young man. He stood at five feet eleven inches, with a caramel-like skin tone. His skin was smooth and silky smooth, and his striking facial features made him look incredibly pretty. He had light brown eyes that looked warm and enticing. His hair was cut into a skin fade that fell nicely with his skin tone, and he had a beard that was shaped but a little scanty in areas, which gave him an edge. Athletically built, he had a tattoo sleeve that covered his whole left arm and another tattoo sleeve that covered his right forearm.

Ava was his escape from the world he ruled; she was the fortress that allowed him to release the child he still was. She allowed him to be him and in a way became the mother he craved. Kenan met her at a friend's barbeque when they were fifteen. Since then, they had become each other's release.

"Yo, young K, you see that fine-ass girl over there? She likes you, player. Go talk to her," an older mentor said to him at that barbeque.

"But how do you know that, G? She don't know you."

"Her friend just told me, nigga. She saw me chatting to you earlier. You gonna talk to that or not, nigga?"

"OK, I'm going, I'm going." Smelling his breath and rubbing his eyebrows, Kenan approached Ava. "Hi, I'm Kenan. May I sit here next to you?"

"Sure, only till that girl over there at the barbeque comes back, because that's her seat," she replied, pointing to her friend.

"So, can I get your name?"

"Ava."

"So, Ava, do you have a boyfriend, or are you single?"

"Hmm, you don't waste time, do you? Well, luckily for you, I'm single, but before you ask for my number, I need to ask one question."

"Go ahead, Ava."

"Are you a gangbanger?"

"Me? No, I wouldn't do that."

"You wouldn't lie to me, would you? I don't like liars, so just be honest."

"OK, well, I'm affiliated," he replied, smiling, with his hands over his eyes, which peeped through.

"Well, you can have my number," Ava replied, smiling as she entered her number into his phone.

As time went on, the relationship blossomed, and they grew very much in love. Kenan's wall came down, and he felt extremely vulnerable. He coped with that by becoming controlling and jealous. Once Ava couldn't take it anymore, she left him, and he hadn't loved another girl since.

6

One night, at 7:33 p.m., Cordell was walking home from the basketball park a little nervously. In his neighborhood, if you stayed outside too late, there usually was trouble. He had his headphones in, listening to Kendrick Lamar's "Alright." As he fell in and out of concentrating on getting home safe, his mind was torn between checking every corner and dancing while walking.

Turning the last corner and coming onto his street, he looked up and saw a bunch of red colors. He concentrated on what was in front of him and realized that he saw a bunch of Blood (Piru) gangbangers. Looking even more intently, he saw Kenan and thought, *Naaah, ugh, ugh, I am not chilling late anymore. I know this nigga is going to see me now.*

As Cordell tried to look straight ahead and go unnoticed, Kenan saw him and walked up to him. "What's up, little homie. You cool?" Kenan asked in a smooth tone, starting off the conversation as if it were a lighthearted meet-up.

"Yeah, I'm cool, G, just trying to get home," replied Cordell.

"I see you talking to Ava the other day at the Crenshaw party. You two together, nigga?"

"Nah, we ain't together, my man. We just really good friends, man."

"Aight, nigga. Well, just in case, I'ma let you know that I'm still feeling that, so if you do like her, my man, just know you got competition, and this competition don't lose, my nigga," Kenan replied with fire in his eyes. When Kenan replied with some aggression, Cordell became defensive, as if he had to match Kenan in order to let him know that he wasn't going to be a pushover.

"Yo, I hear you, my man. Just know that she's into me, G, so I'm good with the competition," Cordell stated with some fight in his voice. Cordell thought, *Let me walk past before it gets physical,* and turned into his house, walking past Kenan with some aggression. Kenan smiled, looked to the floor and shook his head, and walked back to the homies.

Cordell knew that from that moment, life was about to get real serious for him. Having time to ponder the exchange with Kenan in the evening, Cordell thought that he might need to stay on the lookout for some retaliation.

The next morning, Cordell got ready and headed off to school. Cordell did not leave his home without music, as music was very important to him. Walking to school listening to Tupac's "I Ain't Mad at Cha," he went past Ava's house.

Ava said, "Cordell, Cordell … Ah, man, he's got headphones in," and ran in order to catch up.

Cordell sensed someone was behind him, so he looked back. Noticing Ava, he took his headphones out. "What'up, girl? You good?"

"I'm straight. I was just running out 'cause I'm late for my early writing class. Why you so early, though, mister?"

"Ah, me? I'm just going to the library to work with Mr. Columbo on my English essay and avoid some drama."

"What drama, Cordell?"

"Well, your crazy-ass ex-boyfriend, what's his name …

erm … Kenan? We had a little talk, and now, I'm in a position where I'm fighting for you. You need to talk to that nigga because I don't want those types of problems right now."

"I'm gonna talk to him. You know, I know, and that nigga knows that I want you, not him."

"Well, I'm glad to hear that, but that crazy-ass dude needs to hear that shit, foreal, Ava. Foreal." Ava grabbed Cordell's hand and bumped him and smiled. Cordell could not resist and smiled back.

Entering school, Ava made her way to writing class, and Cordell went to see Mr. Columbo. There, Mr. Columbo told him, "Cordell, your writing style is incredible. You are definitely talented. I do not need to make any corrections; just stay focused, and do not let the culture of the neighborhood get you. You have a bright future."

"Yes, sir, I'm focused, Mr. Columbo." Cordell knew he was gifted at writing. He had started writing stories at seven years old. He thought of it as a different form of rapping, telling stories of what he saw in Baltimore and New York. He compared himself to Tupac, Biggie, Snoop Dogg, and Nas; he thought if he could tell stories that were just as vivid and undiluted as those guys', he would have success writing novels. He loved all these artists ability and understood why he liked them. He loved Nas's rawness, the way Tupac could put sentences together, and both Biggie's and Snoop Dogg's delivery and how their words sounded together; they all made their stories sound real, making them relatable for the audience. Unfortunately, Cordell knew he couldn't rap; he didn't have the natural ability for it and thought that novels and short stories and the occasional script came to him more naturally.

Cordell was currently writing a novel based on his

brother's story. Mr. Columbo was transfixed by the story and was always on Cordell's case. Cordell appreciated the push; he knew he needed it sometimes.

"Yo, Cordell, where you been at, man?" Jayden asked mischievously, trying to banter Cordell.

"I was just with Mr. Columbo working on some English work," Cordell replied smugly.

"Oh, foreal? I never knew that nigga set more work."

"Nah, he didn't; he just gave me extracurricular work."

"Oh foreal, you always doing something to be better. I like that, homie."

As Jayden was talking, Cordell said to himself, *I hope Jay and Marcel won't be offended when I tell them about the book.* Cordell spoke to them about everything but he never mentioned the book to them. He considered them brothers to him, so he never wanted to upset them. Marcel and Jayden were both transparent when they were altogether but he kept this from them – guess it was his own little close harbored secret.

In order to change the subject and inform Jayden of the confrontation with Kenan, Cordell said, "My *niggaaa* … Jayden, you'll never guess what happened to me last night, man."

"What happened, homie?"

"I bumped into Kenan last night, and we had a small conversation about Ava."

"Nigga, I told you he was still crushing on her. You gotta do something to get out of this, 'cause if that nigga catch you with her again, my nigga, you gonna need some form of protection. Do you want me to talk to my cousin in Crenshaw, 'cause he could look after you, homie."

"Nah, nigga, I'm good. I know the streets too. If he really wants shit, we could pop off, nigga."

"Homie, I'm on your side too. If you need me, I'm here, nigga, me and my cousin … But you a crazy-ass nigga, homie."

Having grown up in neighborhoods that were troubled by crime, violence, gang culture, drugs, and adolescent sex, Cordell knew what it took to be a street man. After his brother was murdered, his brother's friends in Baltimore had looked out for Cordell and taught him the streets but made sure he never ever became one of them. Now, Cordell thought, *How different could it be out here in LA?*

7

A few weeks had gone by since Kenan and Cordell's confrontation. In that time, Cordell had nearly finished writing his book, and Kenan had stayed very busy making money and running his Piru crew.

Kenan rolled up with his crew at the weekly Crenshaw street party, coming out of the car with two other young men. He was feeling himself; he looked good, as usual, but there was a glint in his eyes today. This normally meant trouble.

Ava hadn't been able to get to Kenan in the past few weeks because whenever she tried to reach out through messages he wouldn't reply, so she wanted to speak to him tonight at the Crenshaw party. "Kenan ... Hey, Kenan, I know you hear me. I need to talk to you!" Ava shouted when she saw him.

"What's good, Ava? I know what you're here for—you've seen me just now and want me back. I know; it is the best choice for all."

"Nigga, you feeling yourself a bit much?" she replied with attitude. Ava couldn't stand having to talk to him. She looked at him now and just hated the fact she had ever formed any kind of relationship with him. Yes, she thought he was extremely good-looking, but because she knew him and what he could do, she couldn't see past his violent acts. "Who are you to go threatening Cordell because you cannot understand that we are over, done, nada, nothing, nigga? Leave him alone, and leave me alone. I'm not yours. Go find another girl, OK? I like Cordell."

And with that last statement, Kenan's blood began to boil. "What do you mean you like Cordell? He ain't shit. What can that nigga do that I can't, huh? You know that nigga ain't got nothing on me."

"He's got a lot more going for him than you do. When you grow up, you'll understand how much more he has got going for him, you dumb-ass nigga." And with that, she walked away. Cordell wouldn't show up this Friday, and it was good that he wouldn't. Tension was now brewing, and you could have cut the atmosphere with a knife.

Just arriving was Jayden. He drove in alone and made his way to his other friends, passing Kenan in order to meet up with his friends. Kenan called him back. "Jayden."

Turning around, Jayden saw who it was, and a thought ran through his head: *Ah, this nigga. I'ma clock your ass if you try me, nigga, and my cousins here too.* "What's up, Kenan?"

"Just chilling, nigga. Forget that. Your homie Cordell … he's treading in deep waters, my nigga. Tell him to stay away from Ava, or else he will not like what comes next."

Stepping forward, Jayden replied calmly but surely, "Whether Cordell stays away from Ava or makes her his girlfriend, you ain't gonna do shit, my nigga. Ava don't want you, homie, so you need to move your ass on."

"Who do you think you are stepping to, nigga? Do you know who you're talking to? Do not make me have to turn this shit ugly, nigga, 'cause I'm on my last nerve," Kenan replied, showing his handgun to Jayden by lifting up his top.

As Jayden was backing away with his hands up, Jayden's

cousin came rushing over with his boys, saying, "Do we have a problem, nigga? Do we have a problem?"

Kenan smiled and shook his head, replying, "Nah, homie, there's no problem. We're just playing, ain't that right, Jayden?" Jayden just started at him in silence. Kenan walked away with his boys and said to Jayden, "I'll be seeing you, my nigga!"

As all of this transpired, Ava shook her head and realized that she and Cordell were in real trouble. While she went through emotions of fear, anger, and anxiousness, she trembled at the thought of what could happen to Cordell because of her; she didn't know what to do. She guessed she could only turn to God now.

8

Ava knew God through her mother. Ava's mother had a rough childhood and found God in her early teens, just before she had Ava. Ava grew up in the church and was a member of the choir. She had an angelic voice; it hit people's ears with a sweetness that made hearts melt. Her voice could open the hearts of the strongest men. God definitely blessed her with a gift, and she knew it, and everyone else who heard her sing knew it.

Innocence was Ava's name, and naïveté was her leader. She had not been with any man. Even Kenan had not touched her, and that was the reason why he knew she was so special. Also, she knew what she wanted from life and was definitely going to get it. However, home was not as sweet as she'd like. Her father was hooked on heroin, and all her mother did about it was pray. Ava thought that kicking her father out of the home would have been better for everyone.

Going for Kenan helped take the pain away and distract her. Kenan represented the type of father she would have wanted—strong, authoritative, and charming. He had something she had never experienced, and she didn't know how to go to God and see Him in that way because she didn't understand where love from a man came from. She knew she had value of some sort but couldn't really identify it in its entirety. Ava looked confident on the outside, but she had her issues. She felt angry—angry at what her father had become and at what she saw as her mother's weakness. Ava usually directed her anger at Kenan or the other girls Kenan was associated with. In one case, she said, "Wait, Kenan. Who is this you're with now, nigga?"

"Hold up, Ava. Why are you always coming on a confrontational tip. How you know she ain't my nigga's girl?"

"Nigga, please. I know you, and I know she isn't your nigga's girl, because you introduced her to me, you dumb-ass nigga. I'm sick of this shit, you cheating-ass nigga. You a ho, nigga; I hope you know that."

"Ava, you trippin'. I ain't doing shit, man. This bitch is crazy, yo." Ava's instinct was to throw something, and that's exactly what she did. She threw the glass that she had picked up, and it grazed his shoulder, cutting it as it shattered. "Ava, are you crazy? That could have been so much worse."

"I don't care, and you better get your side girl up and out of here before I beat her ass."

"Helana, you better go before she does something crazy," Kenan told the other girl.

"OK, K, I'll let you and this ho talk."

"Ah, hell nah, she did not just call me a *ho*. Kenan, you better get her, or else it's about to get real up in here." Before he could turn around, Ava jumped at the other girl, grabbing her hair and dragging her to herself. She punched her in the throat and then slapped her and rushed at Kenan and kneed him in his private area. After observing Ava's one-woman destruction, the other girl left.

Ava left Kenan after she caught him cheating. His controlling and cheating ways had chased her away, and she needed to find a new comfort. She found that in Cordell.

9

Ring-ring! Ring-ring! Cordell's phone was ringing. "What'up, Jay?"

"I'm good, my nigga. We about to hit the court. Just phoning to know whether you good to get over here."

"Yeah, man, where you at—the park?"

"Yeah, we at the park, and Ava and her girls are here too; they're watching. You need to come and impress your girl," Jayden replied, jokingly laughing.

"Aight, homie. Give me five minutes, my nigga."

Arriving on the scene, Cordell went over to Ava and her girls and greeted them and then went over to the boys to get warmed up and play. "Jayden, did you use the baby lotion I gave you?" Cordell asked sarcastically.

"Yeah, I did. Why?"

"Then why are your knees so ashy, nigga? I hope you brought long socks to cover them up, nigga," Cordell replied, laughing along with all the other boys.

"Nigga, you want to get at me with your ashy lips, homie? I hope you don't kiss your momma with those lips, nigga. And you even went over to Ava with those lips, nigga? You have no shame," Jayden replied, laughing and joking with the other boys also.

As the game got started, the teams seemed even in

ability. All the boys were in good condition, looking athletic and quick. Marcel was by far the best player on the court, but Cordell and Jayden were also good at basketball. Cordell and Jayden didn't like being on the same team. They loved competing with each other and gave each other funny trash talk.

Cordell got the ball from Marcel at the top-left side of the key, guarded by Jayden. "What's up, Jay? You ready to get dunked on, my nigga?"

"Nigga, you can try, but it ain't gonna happen."

"Jay, where you want me to go, left or right?"

"Go right."

While this conversation was going on, Cordell was holding on to the ball. Cordell then jockeyed to the right and went left, bypassing Jayden, and then Euro-stepped between two others and laid it up into the basket. "Jayden, you can't touch me; I'm too quick and strong and skillful. What you got, my nigga? I think you need to go sit down."

"Cordell, keep talking, my nigga. I'ma dunk on you and make you my poster boy."

As the game continued, it became more and more competitive. Dunks here, layups there, and a few three-pointers went up.

As the game began to wind down, Kenan and four of his followers came around and sat with Ava and her girls, talking and harassing them. Approaching Ava, Kenan demanded a hug. "Ava, I've missed you. Where you been at?"

"Kenan, not now. I don't want to hug you. We are not together, and we are definitely not friends, so go away and leave us alone."

Kenan still tried anyway, pulling Ava to him and trying to grab a good hold of her. Ava was struggling to push him away, trying to break free. When it turned into a little scuffle, Ava began to shout for help.

As Ava shouted, the game stopped, and the ball began bouncing away from Marcel's grip. At first, everybody stood frozen. Then, Cordell ran over with a speed that not even he knew he possessed and pushed Kenan away with force. Cordell, standing at six feet two inches, was three inches taller and also weighed more than Kenan, so that affected his strength in comparison to Kenan's. Kenan came back and punched Cordell in the chest and thigh, and then Cordell punched Kenan's left cheek with his stronger right hand, making Kenan stumble backward.

Kenan's friends ran over at Cordell, and Cordell hit the first one, stumbling him to the floor, while the others smothered Cordell. As they smothered Cordell, Jayden, Marcel, and the rest of the boys ran over and got them forcefully off Cordell, beating them up and stamping on them. As Kenan found his footing and noticed one of his friends knocked out on the floor from Cordell's punch and the others smothered by the boys, he brought out his gun and shot it in the air twice. Everybody then scattered and ran for their lives.

After all the commotion, Kenan and his friends were left in the park. Kenan walked over to his friends, shaking his head in disappointment, to help them up and look after their friend Isaac, who was now gaining consciousness.

What had stopped Kenan from directing a bullet at someone? He knew that most of the boys there had gang affiliations, and he didn't need a war right now, with the state of his drug business. His drug business was doing well at this point. Having a war and losing the good men making him money would not be a good thing. Replacing them would be hard. Also, all the gang members Cordell and his boys knew were not from the neighborhood, and he didn't know how far they were willing to go to protect Cordell and the boys. Cordell was protected by Jayden, whose cousin was a known Blood member and leader of his own small gang that was known for enjoying violence and murder. However, Kenan knew he had to address this in order to maintain his leadership and image. A war was brewing.

10

"Yo, my nigga, did you see that? Naaah, G, did you see that?" stated Cordell.

"Homie, we were in it. That was crazy, my nigga. I can't believe that happened," replied Jayden.

At this point, the whole crew was split up due to the shots Kenan had fired. However, everybody had run for cover in areas from which they could all see the park court. Jayden, Marcel, and Cordell ended up in the same place, watching Kenan and his boys arguing about the situation.

"Eh, did you see me put Kenan on his bum? Nigga can't handle my hands."

"I saw it, C, but the dude did hit you twice first, my G," Jayden stated.

"Yeah, but he hit me in the chest and thigh, which—I ain't gon' lie—hurts. Well, now it does; now, I can feel it … But I hit him once, and nigga went stumbling to the floor."

"Yeah, homie, I saw that. Had nigga tripping on shoelaces, nigga," replied Marcel.

"Y'all niggas had my back, though. Good looking out," said Cordell.

"We got you, homeboy … But y'all know we just started a war with Kenan, right?" asked Marcel.

"Yeah, now we're gonna need some heat, especially me. I live real close to the nigga," explained Cordell.

"Well, I'll speak to my cousin. That nigga hates Kenan, so he'll deffo wanna help in this thing going on," expounded Jayden.

"Yeah, homeboy definitely wants to get his hands on Kenan for what he did to your little cousin," publicized Cordell. The little cousin Cordell was talking about was the young man Kenan tied to a chair and fed to his pit bulls.

11

"Yo, my nigga. We about to be menaces in this bitch. No way are those niggas gonna get away with that shit, especially Cordell. That nigga is dead, my nigga!" shouted Kenan.

"Nigga, what about Marcel, though? We getting him?" asked Raymond. Now, Raymond asked knowing and respecting the fact that Marcel could get out of the hood and do amazing things. He could show and remind the younger ones that they could get out of this system that kept them feeling as if they had no hope. Many young black men and women never actually made it out of the hood to do amazing things, so the cycle would repeat itself—grow up, gang bang, have kids, sell drugs or take drugs, and die. This was the cycle.

"Nah, Marcel's going to the league. Let him go. We need some grown folks for these little niggas to look up to," replied Kenan.

"But what if that nigga tries to get all fresh and shit? I ain't having that. I'ma shoot the chump." Isaac stated in jealously.

"Nigga, do what you need to. I just want to get that fool, Cordell." Replied Kenan not bothered to argue with Isaac.

"They'll be at the Crenshaw street party on Friday next week. We can get them then." Raymond stated.

"Nah, homeboy, we gotta be smart about this. Let's get them when they're relaxed. They'll be expecting a reaction. We'll just wait till we know those niggas think we ain't gon' come for them, and then, *bam*—we'll peel those niggas' caps back, my nigga," replied Kenan.

"Yeah, my G, that's right. We hit 'em when these niggas aren't looking."

On Friday, as Cordell stepped out the house onto the front porch to enter Marcel's car, Cordell and Kenan caught each other's eyes. Cordell stood on the step, realizing this stare-down meant something. Kenan raised his head from his friend's car window to then stand straight and glare back, also realizing that this was not a typical stare-down. Cordell puffed his chest out and scrunched up his face to show that he was ready for what was about to happen. The tension was so strong that the others involved began to realize what was going on. Kenan's boys stood and looked too, and Marcel looked over at Kenan from the car. Kenan then nodded twice and smiled, turning back to his friend in the car and shaking his head. Kenan was thinking, *This nigga doesn't know who I am .He has no idea what I am capable of. I can't wait to get him.*

Cordell then made his way to Marcel's car and got in, greeting all within it. "What'up, homies? Y'all straight?"

"Yeah, my nigga, we all straight. You straight?" replied Jayden.

"Yeah, nigga, I'm straight. Yo, Marcel, let's get out of here." They were driving to the house of Jayden's cousin, Big A. He lived just on the outskirts of Crenshaw.

Arriving at Big A's house, they got out. Cordell stood there, looking left and right, assessing the area. Two of Big

A's friends were sitting on the steps of their house across the street and watching him, trying to clock his face. "Eh, yo, nigga, you lost? Where you from, nigga?" shouted one of them.

Then Big A stepped out of his house and shouted, "Nah, he cool, my nigga! Let him be, G." Acknowledging what Big A said, the young man who shouted sat back down to carry on his conversation.

Big A was a Blood (Piru) too, just from a different area. His younger cousin who used to live with him, whom Kenan killed, had also been a Blood member from Long Beach. The young man Kenan killed had moved here to live with Big A and his mum. Here, Big A's cousin Jayden realized that the gangbanging game had changed, especially when he realized that Big A's best friend was a Crip member and he was sitting there in the midst of Blood members as if he were a Blood. Big A's friends were untouchable in this hood because of Big A.

Big A—whose real name was Arnell—was called Big A because of his height. He stood at six feet five inches and was a little chubby but not fat. He did have a flat stomach but was described as big boned. He had flawless, smooth skin in a dull ocher-brown color. Fresh faced, he had a well-groomed and short Arabic beard similar to Rick Ross's. His facial features were subtle and made him look adorable. Big A had the top of his hair in cornrows, which he put into a man bun, with the rest of his hair in a skin fade. Also, he had tattoos all over—two full sleeves and tattoos all over his torso with intentions of getting his neck worked on.

Big A had been destined to play in the NFL—well, until he got injured in school and couldn't play anymore. Unfortunately, Big A never was too interested in schoolwork, and because he thought he would make it to the big lights, he never bothered learning anything. Once Big A knew it was all over, he decided to choose the streets as his new playground. Big A was born for violence. He enjoyed the adrenaline of shootouts, fights, and trouble. Now, since his cousin had died by Kenan's hands, he saw nothing but red.

"Yo, cuz, who are your two niggas, and what do they want with me, Blood?" asked Big A.

"What'up, cousin. This is Marcel and Cordell. We ran into some trouble with Kenan, and we need some heat, cousin," replied Jayden.

"OK ... So why come to me knowing what you know about me, cousin?"

"Well, I know if we come to you for heat, it ends in us joining West Side Pirus, but we're desperate, cousin."

"Are all y'all ready to join the West Side Pirus?" asked Big A inquisitively. All replied yes. "Now, what are y'all good at? What can you do for the expansion of the West Side Pirus?" asked Big A.

"All of us could do many things; we could do home robberies, sell drugs, and Cordell is definitely good at stealing cars," replied Marcel.

"Aight, all y'all listen, right? We'll deal with Kenan, but till then, y'all gon' be robbing houses for me, right? And Cordell, I want one car to sell every month to start off with, alright?"

"Yeah, that's cool," replied Cordell.

On the way back to the neighborhood, Cordell thought, *What have I just done? I can't live this life. I'm not built to be a gangbanger.* Cordell shook his head. The car was silent. Cordell looked over at Marcel, and Marcel was staring right out the window. *What's Marcel going to do?* Cordell thought. *He is one of the best basketball players in the country at his age and looking to go to college.* This was bad; this was very bad.

What was Cordell's mum going to think? He wouldn't be able to hide this for too long.

"Yo, Cordell, whatever you're thinking, you need to let that go. We've done it now, and you were talking smack about getting heat. We got it now; don't back out now, my nigga," Jayden said.

Cordell looked at him like he was crazy. "Nigga, you know I had to defend myself. I never said I wanted to be a gangbanger, though … What's my momma gonna say when she finds out, G? This shit is messed up, homie."

Marcel looked at Cordell with a look of soberness as if to say, *We've done it; we've got to live with it.* Cordell understood the look and then turned to the window. The car went back to being completely silent.

12

Three weeks had passed since Cordell, Marcel, and Jayden sold their souls to the lifestyle. Jayden was baptized in it, absolutely submerged in the lifestyle, and was beginning to have an attitude that showed he didn't care about anything. Marcel and Cordell were more humble and elusive about it. Marcel still played high-level high school basketball and kept up all his schoolwork alongside gangbanging. Cordell kept working on his writing and was still very serious about his grades alongside the gangbanging.

As Marcel and Cordell walked back from school together, Marcel's phone rang. *Ring-ring.* It was Big A. "Hello?" Marcel answered.

"What'up, my young king. How was basketball practice, my nigga?" asked Big A.

"Yeah, my G, it was aight. What's up, though?"

"Well, we've just seen that nigga, Kenan's man, that Isaac nigga that said he wants you, my nigga. What you wanna do? He gonna be here all day, so you can come meet me and Jayden at the game store on the corner with Cordell, and we can get him."

"Yeah, nigga. We'll be there in, like, thirty minutes, my nigga."

"Cool. Bring that heat, my nigga." Big A cut the phone.

Marcel turned to Cordell and gave him a look that said *It's about to go down.*

"Marcel, what's popping?" asked Cordell.

"We gonna meet A and Jayden at the game store to get that nigga that's after me, Isaac man."

"Aight, man, I'ma get my balaclava. Don't forget yours, nigga. You got ball to think about, G," replied Cordell.

"Cordell, I got mine on me now, my nigga. I gotta be extra careful," replied Marcel. Both of them, Cordell and Marcel, had been in situations where they needed to shoot, but Cordell had missed on purpose because he wasn't able to leave a woman childless. But Marcel never missed and never felt anything when he did it. The three boys were becoming the stereotypes they never wanted to become.

Thirty minutes had passed, and by this time, Marcel and Cordell had both joined Jayden and Big A. They both got into the car with Jayden and Big A and watched him from there.

It started getting dark, and everybody besides Kenan's friend and the store manager left. Nudging Cordell in order to wake him up, Marcel acknowledged that Kenan's friend was leaving. He stated, "Yo, Cordell, get up, man. The nigga is leaving." Cordell put the balaclava on properly, completely covering his face, believing all of them would do the hit.

"Yo, Cordell, since you're closest to the door, get out and do it, nigga," Big A stated. Cordell looked up at Big A as if he wanted him to confirm it. "Nigga, get out, and do it before the nigga gets away, fool!" shouted Big A.

At this moment, Cordell realized that he had to do it and he had to do it alone. He felt numb. He recognized the depth that he had to go to in order to perform the act of murder. He knew that if he didn't do it, he'd most likely lose his friends. If he did, he'd have killed one of his own people, and if he did it and missed, Kenan and his friends would realize that they had performed the hit, and they would retaliate at him first. Cordell could really shoot. He would never have missed the shots he normally missed if he just had it in him to kill. But today of all days, he had to kill, and he had to do it right. He looked inside himself and allowed himself to be submerged in the hate for Kenan he kept controlled.

As Kenan's friend reached for the door of the building and took his first steps to the car he came in, Cordell finished putting the silencer on his .500 Smith & Wesson magnum pistol. Cordell waited for Kenan's friend to turn his whole body toward his car; then as he turned, Cordell popped open the car door, jogged over to Kenan's friend, and shouted, "Break yourself, nigga!" As Kenan's friend turned around, Cordell shot four bullets. *Pop, pop, pop, pop!* The bullets hit Kenan's friend in the head just above the right eye, twice in the chest—the first around the heart and the second in his left lung—and directly in the stomach. Nobody noticed a thing, as the silencer worked perfectly. Kenan's friend was hit. Cordell ran back into the car.

Big A realized that Kenan's friend was crawling to his car; he had heart. "Yo, Cordell, give me your gun. Nigga got heart." Cordell turned to Kenan's friend and ran back out without remembering Big A wanted to finish the job.

"Yo, nigga, turn around. You think you got heart, huh, nigga?" Cordell stated.

Kenan's friend turned around and said, "Do it then, nigga," and Cordell shot him three more times. *Pop, pop, pop!* All the shots fired landed in his head. Kenan's friend was definitely dead this time. Cordell ran into the car. Big A drove off slowly as if nothing had happened. Nobody saw or heard a thing, anyway, so there was no need to draw attention to themselves by speeding off.

Cordell removed the balaclava and looked at the other guys. Big A was behaving normally, as he did this all the time, but Jayden and Marcel looked at Cordell differently than usual. A look of fear gripped them. Cordell saw Jayden as the one who embraced the new culture with open arms, but Cordell seemed to have grabbed their attention. Something in Cordell changed that day. It wasn't the fact he performed the act of murder; it was the way he did it. Anger seemed to have wrapped Cordell around its finger in that when he didn't kill perfectly the first time he fired the shots, he told the guy to turn around so he could look into his eyes before he killed him. Though Marcel and Jayden had killed in the three weeks since they joined, they had never killed like that.

Cordell turned from their looks and looked straight out the window. Something had definitely clicked inside him.

13

The next day after the events of the shooting, Cordell's doorbell rang, setting off the sweet little bird tweeting sound the bell always made to signify that someone was at the door. Cordell's mum was in the kitchen making collard greens and barbeque chicken. "Cordell, the door!" she shouted.

Cordell opened the door to see Ava standing there. He took in the Beyonce Heat fragrance that she had on as the wind softly blew into his face when he swiftly opened the door. He loved that fragrance; that's why he bought it for her. He then took in Ava's appearance. He was definitely infatuated with her; she was absolutely gorgeous. He loved her sweet smile the most, but this time, she wasn't smiling. He hadn't seen Ava in a while, and though they were technically still friends, they both knew what each of them really wanted even if they didn't say it. She was suspended in the doorway; something was truly wrong with her. This was something Cordell hadn't experienced. She was upset about something.

"Erm, are you just going to stand there and look at me, or are you going to let me in?" she said rhetorically with an irritated undertone. Realizing what she said, he quickly moved out of the way so she could come in. "Mhm, your mum is cooking up a storm," she declared as she smelled the sweet aroma of the food.

"Yeah, Momma is cooking. She's always doing something in that kitchen," he replied.

"I'm going to say hi to your mum. Hey, Ms. Callwall. How are you?" Ava asked respectfully.

"Hey, Ava. I'm well, thank you. Yourself? How's Momma?"

"She's good, I'm good—thank you. You're cooking up a storm in here, aren't you?" Ava stated, smiling.

"Yeah, girl, you're welcome to stay and join us for dinner if you want."

"Oh yes, please, I'd enjoy that. Your cooking is the bomb."

"Well, I'm pleased to have you, and thank you, girl," Cordell's mum stated with a little chuckle. Ms. Callwall liked Ava. She quickly noticed that Ava was different from all the other girls in the neighborhood. Ava was considerate, respectful, and gracious—she walked and moved with elegance and spoke with grace, and that was incredibly hard to find in the hood. It was due to how her mother brought her up. Ava's mother was exactly the same; she was also a prayer warrior and a fervent churchgoer, and she truly served God. If anyone was a spitting image of their mother, it was Ava. She took her mother's looks and personality. Ms. Callwall knew Ava was good for Cordell, and she, too, noticed the chemistry and love the two kids had for each other.

Walking up to Cordell's room, Ava took one more deep breath of the food cooking and smiled. Their friendship had blossomed as time wore on, even though Kenan was always trying to persuade her differently. Entering Cordell's room, she took off her Nike Air Jordan 11 Lows and jumped on the bed to lie on it facing Cordell, who sat at the computer desk.

"You and your small feet," Cordell said.

"Leave me and my small feet alone. Look, I got a pedicure. Do you like the color?"

"Well, it's clear, so … what color is there?"

"Oh shhh, do you like it, though?"

"Yeah, it is nice." They joked back and forth.

"So, erm … Why haven't you called me in the last couple days, please?" she asked sarcastically, although she had a very serious undertone to her voice.

Cordell looked at her with a look that could not explain himself. "Well, what happened was … I just got so caught up in writing and basketball and school."

"Don't give me that. I'm sure you didn't just up and abandon Marcel and Jayden because of that, so don't try and pull the wool over my eyes, nigga."

"Why do I have to be a *nigga* now?"

"'Cause you acting like one, nigga."

"Girl, I swear, call me that again, and see what happens."

"*Nigga, nigga, nigga, nigga*—what's going to happen?" she replied with a screwed-up face that turned into a smile.

Cordell got up in a flash and got to the bed and to Ava so quickly you wouldn't be able to say the word *sausage*. He tickled her and pulled her in close and apologetically said, "I'm sorry, A. You know I was thinking about you, though. But don't worry; it won't happen again." Cordell knew he was only human and he wasn't the best with his phone, but he did mean what he said. He loved Ava with everything he had, and seeing her upset made him genuinely upset. He loved it when she smiled and laughed. All he wanted to do was make her happy, and she felt the same. He looked at her, taking in her whole being. He was in awe of her—that was the only way he could simplify the feeling. He thought that she was worth all the hustle and bustle of getting rid of Kenan. He didn't care how he had to get rid of Kenan; he just had to do so he could completely have her without any trouble.

As Ava enjoyed this embrace, and eased into his arms more, she asked with genuine care, "How have you been, though, baby boy? I have really missed you."

"I've been OK, A—just a little stressed at all I have to deal with from school, basketball, and writing." He was lying. He couldn't believe he lied to her. He never thought he would ever have to do that. He shook his head, knowing full well that was not the reason why he felt stressed. Cordell was torturing himself for killing Kenan's friend in cold blood.

At the time, he had totally not been himself. The act of murder was crazy enough to turn the sanest of men bonkers, but the way he did it made him scared of himself. His crew told him the story of how he did it over and over again, and even though he acted like it was nothing to him in front of them, inside, he actually wanted to curl up in a ball and cry till he forgot about it. But was that his last time killing? He was too scared to be honest with himself because he knew the answer was most likely no.

14

K enan was walking up and down Angel's room filled with rage. Tears were dropping down his face. Angel just sat on the edge of the bed gripped by shock, and in that shock, silence and confusion showed from inside him. They had just received a phone call that their friend was shot and killed—had seven bullets in him and had four of them in his head.

This troubled Kenan. He couldn't fathom his friend was shot. He was hurting. He knew this was part of the gangbanging lifestyle, but he never knew they had opposition ready to get them now. "Angel, my heart. Nigga, my heart. Nigga … They took Isaac, my nigga—Isaac, nigga. Why, nigga, why?" Kenan shouted in pain. He had so much pain that it felt like someone was physically tearing his heart, piece by piece.

Isaac was one of the people closest to Kenan. He was sixteen, and his family was one of the poorest in the neighborhood. His parents were hooked on crack cocaine; both had been laid off work and were close to being homeless. Kenan helped buy them groceries and occasionally paid their rent. Because Isaac was good at rapping, Angel and Kenan both paid for studio sessions to help him get out of the hood, but every time he went home after studio sessions, he realized he needed to spend more time with the set on the block slinging coke.

It hit home for Angel that they needed to figure out who was after them. "Yo, Kenan, what about Big A, Jayden's cousin?"

"What about that, nigga?"

"Well, we killed his cousin, remember, from Long Beach?"

"Nigga, nigga, nigga, that fool's behind it," Kenan replied in revelation. "I swear I'ma get that nigga Angel, but we need proof."

"Well, on Friday, he'll definitely be on Crenshaw," Angel replied.

Kenan looked at Angel, and he smiled and said, "Payback is a bitch, my nigga."

15

Marcel, Cordell, and Jayden were all at Ava's house with Ava and her friends in different places within the house. Jayden and Nicole were in the living room. Marcel and Selina were in the kitchen, and Cordell and Ava were in Ava's room.

"Cordell, we're not going to Crenshaw on Friday, OK?" Ava told him in her room. "I want to see the new King Kong movie away from the neighborhood."

"Ava, when did you start ordering me around, please? This is really new."

"The cheek! I just don't want to go, and I want to spend time with you. Is that OK?" Ava replied with sincerity.

Cordell caught on to what Ava wanted, and that was to get something off her chest. "Ava, what's really wrong?"

"Cordell, I'm tired. I'm really tired."

"What are you tired about, baby?"

"I'm just sick and tired of the same thing. I can't take it anymore, Cordell. I just can't," Ava stated with tears and pain.

Cordell quickly went over to her and held her. He kissed the top of her head and looked at her and said, "Baby, what are you tired of? What can't you not take anymore? What's making you cry, baby?"

"This life, the hood! Why are we here in this hellhole? Why do we, as black people, hate ourselves? Every day, there's either a shooting or a robbery or police in helicopters going around and around. Why do we fight each other over colors and area codes, over drugs and money—Kenan? I'm fed up. I want to leave." Cordell looked shocked as she sobbed in his arms. He had never stopped to ask himself those questions; he was utterly lost for words.

"Isaac got shot, Cordell. Isaac, that poor kid—he was so cute, and he was good at rapping. His mum was in tears at the scene. They knew he was their ticket out." Cordell shriveled up at the statements he was hearing. He couldn't believe the facts that were coming out of Ava's mouth. "Cordell, are you OK, baby? You seem like you've seen a ghost," Ava said.

"Yeah, girl, I just didn't know those things about little Isaac."

"Yeah, he was talented, Cordell. I hope they catch the killer, but can we see the movie away from the neighborhood, baby?"

"Yeah, baby, we can."

16

When Friday came and school was over, as the new usual, Jayden didn't show up to school but Marcel and Cordell attended. But this Friday was different.

Ring-ring! Cordell's phone was ringing. "Hello?"

"Hey, big head. Pick me up at seven. OK, Cordell?" Ava stated with excitement.

"Yeah, that's cool. I'll be at yours by seven." Cordell had his plans with Ava, and Marcel had his plans to go to basketball training. Jayden was the only one going to the Crenshaw street party. He met up with Big A, and they both went to Crenshaw with three other young men. After the shooting of Kenan's friend, Raymond, Big A was extremely smug, knowing he and the others got away with it. Kenan knew they had done it but couldn't prove it; however, today would be his day to get them back. He would provoke a reaction so he would have the right to do something to them.

Big A dressed to the nines. He certainly looked good. He could dress well, but today, he wanted to get some extra attention, and also, he wanted to look at Kenan and rub it in his face that he was untouchable. Kenan and Angel and their crew were already there when he parked up near the rest of his boys and got out with Jayden and the others.

There was extreme tension in the air—so thick that you

could cut it with a knife. At Big A's arrival, the tension only grew. All somebody needed to do was look at Kenan's face to realize something was definitely going to happen. On both sides, guns were present and egos were ready to put themselves on the line. The pressure was incredible; it felt as if a pressure cooker was reaching its boiling point.

As time passed, the evening's tension was still evident. Everybody was on edge, ready to see what would happen. Big A wandered away from the group to chase a young lady. She dragged him to a quiet spot on Crenshaw; as they spoke and exchanged numbers, Kenan and Angel walked past, and Kenan purposely bumped into Big A.

"Nigga, are you OK? Can't you see me standing here, nigga?" Big A asked in disgust.

"Nah, homie, I never saw you. Angel, did you see this nigga standing here?" Kenan asked in a sarcastic tone with a real venom.

"Yo, Kenan, I never even noticed this nigga standing here ... But now you point it out, I just realized how rude this nigga is, asking a question with that tone," Angel stated.

"Yo, Angel, you right, my nigga. I think we should show this nigga what happens when you speak outta tone with us and kill our homie, Raymond," Kenan stated. They both looked at Big A with very serious faces. Then Angel threw the first punch, staggering Big A backward, and then Kenan added a punch, flooring Big A. Both Angel and Kenan could hold their own, but together, they could take anyone down. Kenan was just vicious when he wanted to be, and with his temper, he added to that viciousness; no one could stop him when he saw red. As Big A lay on the ground, Kenan and Angel began stamping him out and beating him with their fists.

Jayden asked one of the crew members, "Where's A?"

"Yo, Jay, I ain't seen that nigga all night, homie," the crew member responded.

Jayden began to panic. He looked around frantically, taking in every nook and cranny of the area. Then he saw Big A getting battered, and he shouted to the crew, and they all ran over and got Kenan and Angel off Big A. Jayden somehow grabbed Kenan and dragged him to the side. Throwing Kenan down to the ground, Jayden stomped on him, punched him, and kicked him, and others joined in when they saw it. Kenan's crew saw and rushed over, and all hell broke loose. Nothing was going to break this up.

After five minutes, police sirens drew near, and two police cars soon surrounded the fight. Once the cars parked, the boys realized the police's presence, and they all dispersed.

17

It had been a few days after the Friday Crenshaw party "Cordell, you and Marcel missed it, man. It went down, my nigga, foreal," Jayden stated with a lust for life.

"Why, what happened?" Cordell stated, fascinated.

"Homie, Kenan got stomped out by me, my nigga. They tried punking on Big A, the homie, so we flew over and stomped him out straight, my nigga."

"Y'all doing the most, nigga? Big A can handle his big ass by himself, nigga."

"Nah, nigga, it don't work like that, my nigga. Big A is the big homie. He can't get it like that. Them niggas need to show some respect, homie, 'cause they can get it too, my nigga."

"You right, Jay, but just know that you need to watch your back now because Kenan ain't playing, nigga."

"Yeah, so what? Forget that, nigga. Are you scared of that nigga, Cordell—the nigga you dropped with one punch? You scared, homie?"

"Nah, nigga, I ain't scared of Kenan or anyone, homie. I just think you need to be careful out here, my nigga."

"Word, homie. I hear you, my nigga."

At this point, Cordell realized that he had to watch his words around his contemporaries. He now saw that he couldn't even be honest with Jayden. Looking into Jayden's eyes, he realized that Jayden was completely lost to the life now—nothing would bring him back. At least he still had Marcel. Marcel could still be himself when he was at school and at basketball and when he was alone with Cordell. Although Cordell stayed quiet and closed around their fellow gang members, Marcel was able to play the game, and when he was around the gang, he acted exactly like them.

Only Cordell still had his inner child and innocence. Even though he killed Isaac in cold blood, he still held that over his heart. He was still a good kid, undiluted. But how long did he have before the streets really got him?

18

Wednesday evening - it had been five days since the incident on the past Friday. Jayden, Big A, and the homies were playing dice outside Big A's house while talking about the events that happened on Friday. None of them knew Kenan and Angel were stalking them, watching them play dice from across the road. Kenan and Angel were parked forty yards away from the house in a Toyota Camry, which they used for hits, as the victims of their shootings never suspected to be hit from a Toyota Camry. With the lights switched off and the windows all the way up, they went unnoticed. Unable to see them, Big A and the boys were laughing and cussing and making references to what they did to Kenan and his crew.

As the game came to an end, the dude with the least money had to go to the store to get beer. In this case, all of them except Jayden went; this couldn't have been a better time for Kenan, while it was the worst time for Jayden. Kenan and Angel were strapped up and ready to bring chaos and violence. As everyone else walked off to their destination to buy alcohol, Jayden sat on the stairs leading up to the front door. Taking his gun out of his waist to be more comfortable, he placed it on the stairs next to him. He took his phone out to phone Nicole. *Ring-ring!* "Hey, baby. You straight? Where you at?" Jayden asked with love in his voice.

"Bubba, I'm at home with Ma just having some girl time, talking about you," she replied. Jayden could tell she was smiling.

As the conversation continued, Jayden had no idea what was coming. Kenan and Angel were waiting for Big A and the homies to turn the corner. "Yo, Angel, when these niggas turn the corner, count to twenty out loud, and when you hit twenty, we sneak up on this nigga and shoot this fool," Kenan said.

"Nigga, I got you."

Once they turned the corner and were out of sight, Angel started the countdown. "Twenty," Angel said. They both came out of the car, leaving the doors open so they didn't alert Jayden and so they had a quick getaway. As they got closer, their hearts were beating with adrenaline—their palms sweaty under their rubber gloves and intent brimming in their eyes.

Emerging out of the blue, Kenan stated, "Break yourself, nigga."

Before Jayden even knew what was happening, gunshots went off. *Pop, pop, pop, pop, pop, pop, pop, pop, pop, pop, pop, pop, pop, pop, pop, pop!* Sixteen gunshots went off—ten hit Jayden. Jayden tried to get into the house, but as he got to the door, he realized it was locked. While banging on the door, he was filled with ten bullets, putting his body into shock. He dropped to the floor shaking. Kenan and Angel had purposely decided not to put on silencers; they did this to send a message. They definitely sent a message. Big A and the homies heard the gunshots and seemed confused for a minute; then they clocked it. They all looked at each other and shouted, "Jayden!" They ran back to the block as if their lives depended on it. Nicole began shouting and crying through the phone.

Angel and Kenan ran into the car and closed the door just as the homies were turning the corner in panic. As they sped off, Big A ran straight to Jayden and held him in his arms, but it was too late. Jayden was dead, his body filled with bullets and in tatters. That was the way of the streets: *Take ours, and we'll take yours, and if you get us, we'll get you.*

19

Cordell, Ava, Marcel, and Selina were all together at a diner having a double date. They were in their own little world.

Ring-ring, ring-ring! Cordell's phone rang. He checked it; it was Big A. As he left it to ring, Ava asked, "Who's that?"

"It's just my cousin," he replied, looking at Jayden.

"Well, if your cousin phones again, pick it up. It could be important," she replied.

The phone rang again. "Hello?" Cordell asked as nicely as he could, considering he didn't want to be on the phone. On the other side of the phone, he just heard sobbing. Cordell quickly realized that something wasn't right. "Yo, A, what's wrong? Why you crying, homie?"

"Cordell, man, Jay's dead," Big A said in a mellow, sorrowful voice.

"What do you mean *Jay's dead*!" shouted Cordell with rage, sadness, surprise, and shock all in his voice at once. At this point, the eyes of Marcel, Selina, and Ava were on Cordell. The atmosphere of the date changed. It went from delightful to despairing in seconds.

"Jay is dead, Cordell—dead. I held him in my hands, C.

He didn't open his eyes once. I couldn't get him to fight it. I couldn't say good-bye. He's dead, C."

At this point, Cordell began to cry. He was glued to the spot. Tears flowed slowly but surely. The pain of loss began to set in. He was experiencing such bitter sadness that he couldn't hear anyone. His friend who was like a brother to him was gone; he was reliving his time in Baltimore, where he lost his blood brother. His heart ached, and his spirit yearned to scream. At this point, Cordell stood in utter gloom, where he felt desolate.

Still, Ava, Marcel, and Selina were in disbelief, crying in their seats. Ava had been with Nicole earlier that night, and neither of them could have seen this happening. Nicole had decided to stay with her mum this evening. Who thought tonight of all nights Cordell and Nicole would lose someone so important to them? They had seen him only yesterday.

20

"Cordell, Ava is here to see you, hun. I'm sending her up!" Cordell's mother shouted with a soft and delicate demeanor the next day. She got no response, so she waved her hand to Ava, stating that she was free to go up and see Cordell.

The door was half-open, but Ava knocked twice anyway and then entered. As she entered, she could feel the sadness in the atmosphere. She could physically feel Cordell's pain, as if she could hold it. "Hey, baby, I just came to check on you ... You haven't answered my calls lately. How are you feeling, baby? Let me know," Ava stated with as much comfort as she could muster while taking off her shoes and crawling into the bed to sit beside him.

"Yeah, I'm all right considering ... I'm better than yesterday," Cordell replied as he looked at her with a smile. Ava was his rock; he couldn't believe that she could be so strong. He sat there looking at her, wanting to know her secret. "Ava, why are you so strong?"

"It isn't me that's strong, Cordell; it's because I rely on God to keep me going."

"I've never heard that before, God making someone strong because of Him," responded Cordell.

"Yeah, but your mother's such a strong believer I

thought you would have recognized that, especially after your brother died."

"I guess I did recognize that, but I didn't allow it to register."

"I got an idea, Cordell. Why don't you come to church with me, and then you'll see for yourself?"

"Erm … I don't know about that," Cordell said, unsure and unconvincing.

"Why not?"

"I don't think God's for me, like, what has He done for me, and how can I serve something that doesn't care for humanity enough to get them out of a situation where the ghetto is killing a people?" Ava looked shocked by Cordell's comments. She didn't know how to conceal her shock. One of her hands was over her mouth while her other hand was on her chest.

Cordell looked at her like she was crazy. He couldn't fathom her shock. "What?" Cordell asked with a confused face.

"OK, God loves us all. He loves you, me, your mother, and everybody on this planet, and those that are yet to come. Why do you love me? It's because you know me, right? God loves us, but He can only help those who turn to Him and get to know Him. He gave us free will to choose Him so we can love Him in order for us to be fulfilled by Him. The ghetto was created by man out of free will because a certain type of person chose to live that way. Why would God solve a problem He didn't create for a people who don't want to change it? So therefore, your statement is not valid, and now, you have to come."

Ava was charged up now. The passion in her voice and the intensity in her eyes spoke volumes to Cordell. He was silenced. He believed. God was pulling on his heartstrings, and he knew it. "Wow, I understand now," Cordell replied as if wisdom just got knocked into him.

"So you're coming to church, then?"

"Yeah, I'll come." In that one conversation, Cordell seemed to have gained back his color and his strength.

21

C ordell had been thinking about what Ava said. She had long since left his home at this point. As he was about to check out his mother's Bible for the first time since his brother's shooting, his phone rang.

"Hello?" Cordell answered.

"Yo, C, you able to meet me at the indoor court? I need some company. My mind is scrambled. I need to shoot or something," Marcel asked.

"Yeah, Marcel, I'll come now," replied Cordell, knowing he, too, needed some air and relaxation after constantly thinking about Jayden.

Cordell got to the gym and saw Marcel there already shooting. Arriving onto the court, he was happy he came. "What'up, homie? You good?" Cordell asked.

"Yeah, C, I'm good. You want to play some one-on-one, C?"

"Homie, I'm down. You may be the best player in the country, but I'll still give you a game."

"G, you talk too much. Show me, nigga."

Once Cordell finished changing, they played rock–paper–scissors in order to determine who would start the game with the ball and who would start on the defensive. Cordell won the rock–paper–scissors; he started on the offensive. Marcel checked Cordell in, and the action began. Holding the ball in his hands, he joked to Marcel, saying, "Homie, you sure you ready for this?"

Marcel chuckled, stating, "Nigga, don't worry about me. I'm the best in the country, remember?"

Cordell smiled and shrugged. Cordell then jockeyed left and went right and laid it up, 1–0 to Cordell. They went on to play seven games. Marcel won four, while Cordell only won three. As they walked over to the benches to sit and get changed, Marcel forgot that Jayden had died and stated with conviction, "We should have called Jayden to come. I could have beat you both on my own."

Cordell looked at him as if Marcel had lost his mind. "Have you forgotten what happened, Marcel?"

"Nah, C. I got lost in the fun we were having and lost sight of why we were even here, man."

"Ah, aight." Cordell let him off the hook this time. They sat and spoke for another forty-five minutes before they left. They spoke about certain memories of Jayden, they cried, they reflected on his humor, and at one point, they both stayed silent. They used this time at the gym to grieve together and grow a deeper bond, remembering Jayden, and it was sweet.

As they were leaving to go to their separate vehicles, they overheard a conversation about Jayden's shooting. When they turned around, they saw Angel and Kenan talking about how they pulled it off to four other young men. Angel was parked close to both Cordell and Marcel. On hearing this, Cordell looked at Marcel with rage and whispered, "We're going to Big A's now."

22

Arriving at Big A's house, Cordell got out of the car, angrily slamming his door as if he wanted to break the windows. He stormed over to the front door and knocked on it as if he were a police officer with a warrant. Marcel was close behind him as the door opened. "Nigga, why are you banging the door like the cops?" Big A angrily asked.

"Nigga, I know who the people were that shot Jayden," stated Cordell with menace in his eyes. Cordell then barged into the house past Big A, and Marcel followed on a quieter note. "It was Kenan and Angel. They did it," Cordell spilled.

"C, we know. We saw their heads get into the getaway car before we could shoot at 'em," replied Big A.

"So what are we going to do to get 'em back?" Cordell asked in urgency.

Marcel looked at Cordell and realized that he was getting caught up in that zone again. Marcel now felt worried because he knew what Cordell was capable of when he got in this zone and Marcel didn't have plans to retaliate. Marcel wanted to move on and get out. "Yo, C and Big, I'm out," he said. "I can't keep doing this—this taking one of them for one of ours. I'm out, man. I need to focus on me and basketball, man."

Cordell looked at Marcel with vexation; he couldn't

believe what he was hearing. To Cordell, Marcel was punking out and forgetting what they had all been through. His blood was boiling, his frustration was showing, and then he said, "*What, nigga!* What did you just say to me? Are you crazy? After these niggas just took your brother, you want to just up and leave it to me and Big? Nah, nigga, you better be down. You can't just leave it to us. I ain't having that, nah, nigga. Big, you hearing this?"

"*Cordell!* Calm down, homie. Don't you get it? M can't do it; he's had enough. Let the nigga go. He's done his share. Leave him to grieve how he grieves, nigga. Me and you will handle this. Marcel, you go home. C will calm down and get with you tomorrow."

"Aight, homie. Big, C, I'm out."

Cordell was hurting, and not having Marcel react the way he did confused him. But he calmed down and realized that not everybody was able to retaliate after losing someone so close, knowing that with retaliation came the other side's retribution. Big A and Cordell talked and planned, and then, after coming up with something, Cordell left for home.

23

Sunday arrived—the Sunday Cordell had reluctantly agreed to go to church with Ava. As he was getting ready, he thought about whether he could find an excuse to get out of it. Unfortunately, he couldn't find a valid reason to wriggle out of this predicament. Considering he felt that he had had something taken away from him, Cordell thought that preachers always went after the congregation's money and there wasn't any truth to what the preachers said.

Ava arrived at the door to pick him up. She looked amazing, as usual. Cordell was anxious; he didn't know what to expect from the service. As they entered the car, Ava asked sweetly, "Are you ready? Are you excited?"

Cordell responded with a practiced smile, saying, "Yeah, I am." Ava saw right through it but gave back her own practiced smile.

Arriving at the church, Cordell was taken aback by how beautiful the building looked. It was something that shouldn't have been associated with the hood. The building stood out like a sore thumb. It was weird, having a building like this in the neighborhood. It wasn't normal; it belonged in Beverly Hills or Manhattan. Walking in, he saw the décor. He looked at Ava with a face of disbelief—Ava smiled at his reaction to the building. She was the same when she first walked in.

Cordell looked around at the people entering the building and was a little shocked that the church was mainly packed with women. It showed that more women are active churchgoers. Looking left, looking right, and then looking behind him, he saw women in their droves. There were men, but the women outnumbered them two to one. Cordell looked at Ava and saw her praying quietly to herself, so he decided to copy her and do the same.

Ten minutes later, the service started. The choir was called up, and Ava left her seat to grab a microphone, as it was her Sunday to lead praise and worship. When she opened her mouth, it sounded as if an angel had taken over her voice. Cordell looked at her with his hand over his mouth; he was shocked that she could sing. He had never heard her sing. In fact, he was close to tears. He knew she was special, but knowing she had a hidden talent heightened his admiration for her. Looking around again, he saw how Ava's leading of praise and worship moved all the congregation. Cordell said to himself, *For this to happen, there must be a God. He made her perfectly with talents far beyond what she probably thinks of them. Thank You, God, for sending her my way.*

Did I really just thank God for Ava? Cordell questioned himself. He had thanked the God of Heaven whose reality he would have questioned yesterday over a song and a girl's voice. Ava was truly talented, though. She would have melted the hardest stony heart with that voice, so it wasn't really a surprise that Cordell was now seeing the God of Heaven through her voice.

The preacher came out and joined in the singing and praising and then called everyone to their seats. As the preaching proceeded, Cordell felt a pull in his heart—he was being spoken to through the Word of God and felt an urge to give his life, but he then remembered his plans with Big A and then remembered Jayden and his brother also. Thinking of those things, he hardened his heart again and was determined to see the end of Kenan.

Cordell showed his feelings in his facial expressions, and Ava was paying close attention. "What's wrong, Cordell?"

"Nothing, Ava. Don't worry. I'm fine—just a little tired."

"You sure, C? I can see you're really not at peace listening, babe."

"Yeah, I'm sure, babe," Cordell replied sweetly in act. She turned and listened to the preaching, and so did he.

An altar call came for those who wanted to be saved. The preacher's words were "Come to the altar. The Father's arms are open wide. Forgiveness was bought with the precious blood of Jesus Christ. He died for you and me. He loves you and cares for you. When you're hurting, He wants to be there for you. Come now, and change your life with the Savior." Cordell wanted to go. His heart was beating, he had tears in his eyes, and he knew God was calling him, but his resentment, hurt, and retribution held him still. One arm was being pulled by God and the other was being pulled by revenge.

Soon, the time for salvation expired. The preacher called for only a few minutes, and those who went received salvation. Cordell missed it. Who knew whether another opportunity like this would arise?

24

It was Friday Crenshaw party time again, and everybody was there, even Ava. Walking along the strip with Marcel, Cordell greeted everybody till he got to Big A. Both Marcel and Cordell then stayed and chilled with the gang. Ava walked over to Cordell and hugged him and kissed him on the cheek and then greeted the others. Kenan saw the whole act and became infuriated. "Yo, Angel, did you just see what she did? Nah, nigga, I ain't having that. I'ma go over there and drag her away from this bummy-ass nigga."

"Cool, G, I'ma let you handle that."

Kenan walked over with intent. Cordell saw him coming and said to the gang, "Yo, yo, yo, Kenan's coming. Let's watch what this nigga does."

Kenan grabbed Ava's hand and dragged her away, talking and shouting at her as if she were his daughter. "Kenan, get off me! You're hurting me," Ava said.

"What do you think you're doing, kissing him on the cheek, that nigga!" Kenan shouted at her.

Ava somehow yanked her arm away and ran back to Cordell and stood behind him. Kenan looked at her and then stared at Cordell. Cordell was now irate; he looked at Kenan with fire in his eyes. Kenan went over and stood right in front of Cordell, looking up to him.

"Cordell, if I were you, I'd move, nigga."

"Why is that, nigga?"

"'Cause my girl is behind you."

"Nah, nigga, she isn't yours, to be honest. She's my girl now, G, so you need to go back to your homeboys, 'cause you look outnumbered right now."

"Nigga, didn't I tell you before, at our last meet, that I always win? Well, today is that day, my nigga, because I ain't moving, homeboy. So I guess we got a problem, nigga, 'cause I know you ain't ready to put them hands up."

"Hmm, is that right, nigga? Try me, my nigga." Cordell stepped forward, towering over Kenan. Big A was standing right beside Cordell and couldn't resist getting involved; he hit Kenan straight in the jaw, knocking him down with one punch. Cordell then turned around, laughed out loud, and walked off with Ava and the gang. Normally, Ava wouldn't have liked being involved in such drama, but because Kenan kept trying to get back into her life, she didn't mind that he had learned the hard way.

Embarrassed and furious, Kenan just had to pick himself up. He walked back to Angel and the gang and stated, "Big A gets it today; we gonna kill that nigga, homeboy." Kenan and the rest of them left the Friday Crenshaw party and went to wait for Big A outside his house.

It was three in the morning, and the Crenshaw party was over. Cordell had dropped off Ava and fallen asleep long before Big A even turned onto his street. Now, Big A parked outside his house, and having called the homies who stayed with him to leave the door open, he jumped out of the car and locked it with the key. Kenan and Angel got out of their car and walked straight to him. They started jogging, and then Big A saw them. When he dashed for the house, Kenan and Angel started shooting. Letting off gunshot after gunshot after gunshot, the boys tried to get him. Somehow, Big A made it into his house without being shot.

Big A slammed the door shut and then jumped to the floor all in one motion. He looked at his body and felt around for any holes and wounds. He luckily found none and saw no blood. After that, he breathed the deepest breath possible and then sighed. He lay there for the rest of the night. A passing thought went through Big A's head: *There must be a God, because I should be dead right now.* But as soon as the thought came, he allowed it to pass just as quickly. The thought that stuck till he fell asleep on the floor was of revenge.

25

Ring-ring! "Hello?" Cordell answered the next morning, whipping his eyes and yawning.

"Nigga, I swear I'ma kill that nigga. I'm gonna kill him!" Big A shouted down the phone with anger and venom.

"Yo, A, it's, like, 7:00 a.m. right now, homie. Who you gonna kill?"

"Nigga, Kenan. Him and Angel came to my house, my nigga. He came to my house and started shooting at me, my nigga … *at me, nigga.*"

"Are you serious, A!" Cordell stated as he jumped up to sit on the bed.

"Nigga, they rolled up on me and just started firing off shots. I had to run and duck and dive into the house. I was lucky the front door was open already and I could get it shut while diving into the house."

"So what are you thinking for the revenge plan?"

"Nigga, I want to get Angel alone, so we are going to wait and really do some surveillance. I want to get him right."

"Homie, I'm down. I got you, my nigga. When you're ready, we'll get this, nigga."

"Cool, my nigga. We gonna talk. Keep safe, my nigga."

"You too, A." As Cordell hung up the phone, he sat

there in silence and really took in what was happening. He had lost Jayden to this needless violence. His closest friend had stopped hanging around him in public and would only be around him if they were playing basketball or their ladies were together. He had nearly lost Big A, and he had killed before and was ready to kill again.

Cordell began crying. His tears were uncontrollable, and his eyes grew red. He looked to the ceiling and questioned God. "What is happening to me, God? Why am I becoming a bad person? Why do I live in the projects? Why did Jayden and my brother have to die? God, how do I change? How do I just leave Big A to face this alone? God, I need you." He sat there in silence.

Cordell realized that he was in a dark place. He looked back at when this trouble started; it started the day he approached Ava. The love Cordell had for Ava was strong. It was a lot stronger than he thought. She was very quickly becoming the woman he thought he'd marry, and he didn't want to give her up so that Kenan, a gangbanging Piru who would eventually end up in prison, would have a chance with her. Ava was beautiful, and her head was tightly screwed on. She was going to become something great in life, and Cordell was too—well, as long as he didn't get caught in his gangbanging activities and murder. He had so far kept it all under wraps from both his mother and Ava, but he was now feeling the pressure due to the loss of his friends. He wasn't ready to lose Big A too, so he was ready to help get rid of Kenan and Angel.

26

Surveillance had taken place for some time now. It was coming up on three months of people following Angel unnoticed. Angel was on the block, waiting for a drop—this happened every second Friday of the month. Angel and a runner no older than fifteen did the drop. Big A, Cordell, and another young man were waiting in a car parked down the street opposite Angel's car. The plan was when Angel walked to his car, they'd all jump him and shoot him. Cordell loved silencers; he never liked unneeded attention. He forced all the other guys to use silencers too because he was a professional. They also had a pretend junkie who was going to approach Angel and keep him busy to distract him.

Cordell was just waiting with his balaclava sitting on top of his head, thinking about their bulletproof plan. When he looked at Big A and the guy at the back, he thought he needed to change his life. It hit him that this was ground zero and the only place lower than this was hell. After looking at them, he took in his environment and then remembered he had a future away from here and being involved in this life was leading him to death—well, eventually. Looking to the ground now, he whispered to himself, "After this, I'm done. I'm out. I'm getting up and out of here and going to college."

The drop had just happened. Big A shouted at Cordell,

76 | Ayodele Olaniyan

"Nigga, look up and watch the nigga! We here for a reason, my nigga. Concentrate." Cordell looked at him with a straight face and then watched Angel.

The pretend junkie stopped Angel from walking past, begging him for some crack cocaine. Cordell put on his balaclava and rolled out of the car with the other two. They crouched down. It was dark, and all three of them were in full black. Angel was so distracted by the junkie he never realized the trap. Cordell then ran up from behind the junkie and stood up and fired two shots all in one motion. The shots hit Angel in his shoulder and neck. He went down clutching his neck.

Big A and the third guy came across and stood side by side with Cordell and the junkie, and Big A said to Angel, "What's good, nigga? You look like you're in a bit of trouble ... See, when you shoot at me, nigga, you better get me. But hey, I guess you have to go to hell first, my nigga. I'll see you there later, nigga." Big A brought out his gun, cocked it back, and then shot him five more times. The shots hit Angel in the head, chest, pelvis, and stomach. Angel was dead, and because of the silencers on the gun there wasn't a sound that could have given away the murder.

Cordell and his friends walked back to the car and drove off. That was it for the night; they were going home in hope of a better tomorrow. Angel had gone to meet his maker and face judgment for eternity. Angel was found the next day at 11:00 a.m.

27

Kenan was an emotional wreck. For weeks, he was inconsolable and full of retribution. Revenge was his motive, and he was driven to get it. He went looking for Big A. Kenan drove around South Central and the outskirts of Compton for weeks on end.

After a month and three weeks, Kenan finally saw Big A coming out of a chicken joint with chicken in his hand, walking to his car. Kenan got the driver of the car he was in to stop, switch off his lights, and then drive as fast as possible. It was time; Kenan was ready to lay down the law on Big A. Big A had caused so much drama and violence that Kenan was ready to end it and end him. Gritting his teeth and holding his gun as tightly as physically possible, he relished the thought of getting him back for Angel's murder. He began smiling as they got closer, the car getting quicker and quicker.

Big A turned around at the sound of the speeding car. It took him a couple of seconds to realize what was happening and who was approaching him. Big A looked closer; squinting, he had a light-bulb moment. He realized that Kenan was sitting on the top of his friend's drop-top convertible, holding a gun at him. Freezing to the spot where he stood, Big A knew this was the end. He thought, *After all these years in the game, I'm going out typically, like a typical nigga.* Big A gritted his teeth and embraced the impact of the gunshots about to fire.

Closing his eyes, he thought about his mother and how he hadn't seen her for years, after she kicked him out for not wanting to stop gangbanging. He then thought of Jayden and how he felt so bad for dragging him into the gangbanging lifestyle when all he wanted was for Big A to handle it. He then turned his thoughts to Cordell. He thought, *I wish I could warn him to just let it go and move on and forget this beef.* His concerns for Cordell were genuine, and he worried that without him, Cordell would get lost in this world and eventually die in the streets.

Kenan stood right in front of him now, and the atmosphere oozed violence. Then gunshots: *Pop, pop, pop, pop, pop, pop!* All six hit Big A. Kenan and his driver sped off.

Big A dropped to the floor, dropping his food. He just lay there, eyes still open. He wasn't dead yet, but he lay there and just relaxed into it, guessing he was ready for this. He exhaled; he could feel the pain, so he chose not to move because of it. His mind went to what would happen when he finally died, and he thought about whether life after death was real. He whispered to himself, "I guess whatever happens will happen. God, if You hear me, I'm sorry. All I did, I now know it's wrong." He cried, adding, "God, I repent. I know You are the Way. I chose to live recklessly, but I realize it is all fleeting. Just remember me here. I'm sorry, God," and then released his final breath.

Big A died with not a soul around him. This was what happened on the streets. As one goes, another replaces them. The hood was a conveyor belt of young gangbangers. It groomed them from a young age, and then, on average, they would die at twenty-five. Big A was a product of his environment. Hopefully, wherever he went now, Jayden would be there.

28

After the phone call, Cordell instinctively threw his phone against a wall in anger and pain at the information he had just received. He went to his knees, covering his face with both hands, tears running down his face. His silent cries were deafening. His heart was broken, his spirit was broken, and his mind was scrambled. He profusely wiped his eyes, and at this point, his tears came thick and fast. He thought, *Again, how many times will I experience loss?* He screamed and screamed and screamed again. Nobody was home, so he didn't have to worry about his mum coming up to check on him.

Losing Jayden and Big A was too much to handle. Big A had become a big-brother figure. Although Big A was not the type of brother figure he embarked on having when he first moved to Los Angeles, Big A had always been there for him. He had Cordell's back in everything.

Cordell finally let it all out and ran out of tears. He wiped his face and went to pick up his phone. It was cracked in three different places, but his screen still somehow worked. Scrolling through his contacts, he typed in Ava's name and called her. *Ring-ring, ring-ring!*

"Hello?" she said sweetly as she picked up the phone.

"Hey, are you busy right now?" Cordell asked solemnly.

"No, baby, I'm free. What's wrong?"

"I need to see you. I'll pick you up in ten minutes."

"OK, baby. See you in ten," she replied with a calming voice.

29

She knocked on Cordell's door. Cordell opened the door and jumped at Ava with an embrace. He held her so tight. She smiled; he sighed. Holding her hand, he led her into the living room. She fell onto the couch and put her feet up on Cordell after taking her shoes off in one motion. "So what's up, baby? You sounded like you were in trouble when you phoned me, Cordell."

"Nah, I'm cool, A … Just wanted to see you. Is that all right?"

"*Please*, I know you, Cordell. Spill the beans. What's up, baby?"

"What's it like serving God and stuff?"

"*Ooh*, you thinking of joining me, C?"

"Well, I think I'm ready to let go and give my life to God. I just want to know from you what it's like to live like that."

"It's amazing, Cordell. The peace and joy I feel daily is what keeps me going in this place we call *home*."

"Wow, you seem so passionate. How do you pray to something you can't see?"

"That's called *faith*, Cordell. It is like I'm talking to you, but I'm talking to God. And just knowing someone like God listens to me—to me, small Ava—keeps me sane."

"Is it true He died on the cross for everybody?"

"Baby, it's so true … He took up our place as a sacrifice to bring us to God, and whoever believes in Him shall be saved, baby." At this point, Ava was speaking with excitement. She wanted him to ask her how to give his life to Christ and become saved, but Cordell was just sitting there, thinking. "So, C, do you want to give your life to God?"

"Let me just think about it. Give me a couple of days." Cordell went quiet, just thinking about his brother, Jayden, and Big A. Tears began to flow slowly.

Ava noticed his retreat and began worrying. "Baby, what's the matter? What's going on with you?"

"Ava, I've lost three people in my life now, all who are— were—close to me. I hate this place … helicopters every night, gunshots nearly every night, constantly having to watch your shoulder, drugs and alcohol. I hate the hood. Why did I have to live here?" Cordell moaned with pain and tears, feeling as if there were no hope of escaping this part of the world.

Ava began to cry as she saw his pain manifest. He was wiping his eyes, but the tears kept coming. The pain of loss, the stress of their environment, and the guilt he felt for seeking retribution weighed heavily on his heart. Ava couldn't help but cry also. She tried to smile at him to see whether that would help him, but seeing her try to comfort him made him feel bad. She couldn't take it; she grabbed him, drawing him close to her, and he held her for minutes on end. They shared something bigger than themselves. They realized at this point that they were really made for each other, and Cordell realized she was there to draw him to Christ. Unfortunately, although he recognized this, he couldn't fully give himself at this point. He still had a little hardness in his heart toward

God, as he believed God should have taken him out of this predicament because he was originally a good kid. Soon, he would realize that he needed God more than he needed Ava.

30

A few months after Big A died, Cordell was willing to go to the regular Friday Crenshaw street party. He had gotten over the grief he felt about Big A's passing and was attending church here and there with Ava. Knowing he didn't initially want to give himself over fully, as he attended more and more, he felt his heart becoming flesh-like little by little. Ava was at her happiest when she knew he was following her to church. Whenever Cordell decided to go to church with Ava, Kenan would get a whiff of this news, and his blood would boil, green with envy. Though Kenan had had that opportunity in the past, he had never showed up to church ever, not once; he knew that church would bring Cordell and Ava closer, and Kenan had to do something that tore them apart.

Before Cordell showed up at the Friday Crenshaw street party, he tried to convince Marcel to go too, as Marcel and Cordell had become close again once Cordell decided to leave the gang after Big A's death. But Marcel wasn't ready to step back into this environment. And Cordell had just decided to come to the party to chill with the same group one last time before he was going to leave for college with Ava in the next four weeks. This was the last time he would step foot in this type of environment.

Cordell greeted the gang, and they greeted him with joy and started joking with him as if he never left. Unfortunately, Cordell didn't know Kenan was after him. Kenan was present, waiting, and watching every move Cordell made.

It was getting late now, and tension was growing, but it didn't come from Cordell. Kenan was walking up and down the strip, following Cordell's movement with a boiling anger that accentuated his true disdain for Cordell. It hit one o'clock, and Cordell was now ready to go home. He said his last good-byes to the gang and walked to his car. As he walked to his car, he remembered all the times he had shared with the gang—hanging out on the block, chilling with the homeboys, stealing cars. He never knew he'd look back and say he actually liked the rush of adrenaline, the parties, and just the brotherhood. He then reflected on the murders of his friends and then the murders he committed. At this point, he shook his head and became distressed. He felt completely sorry and ashamed for what he had done. He knew that murder was a despicable act, and it ate him up every day when it would randomly sneak through his thoughts.

Cordell had parked farther away than usual due to his getting there later than usual. Kenan followed his every step, moving extremely elusively. Kenan was very cunning, and he had Cordell in his sights. As Cordell reached his car and put the key into the door, Kenan ran up behind him and pistol-whipped him so hard Cordell fell to the floor. "Bye-bye, nigga. It's a trip right, nigga? You thought you were gonna drive into the sunset with Ava, nigga? Well, you ain't gonna see her again, nigga," Kenan said as he was stomping him out. Kenan stomped him out for so long that he gave Cordell a few broken ribs and Cordell struggled to move.

Kenan stopped stomping on Cordell and walked back

and forth in a straight line in front of Cordell, talking. "Nigga, I never liked you—like, you were always just in my face all the time. Nigga, today, I'll never see you again. Then we'll see who Ava is with, nigga." He then went back to stomping Cordell out.

After another five minutes, Kenan stopped again and took the safety off his gun. He pulled the trigger, but the gun didn't go off. The bullet was stuck. He pulled it three more times, and nothing happened. The gun was a bad one. Realizing what happened, Cordell somehow found a way to crawl under the car to prevent his getting stomped out again. Kenan stated, "Nigga, I'ma get you, and next time, the gun going to blow, my nigga. Trust me." Kenan looked around to see whether there were any witnesses and then began jogging back to his gang, tucking away the gun.

Cordell crawled back out from under the car and composed himself. He forced himself to get up and then got into his car and sat there with his head on the steering wheel while his right hand was gripping his torso and his left gripped the steering wheel. He replayed what just happened in his head. He started crying. He said to himself, "I nearly just died … I nearly died tonight." As he kept repeating it louder and louder, he began to shout it. He then shouted, "I'm sick of this shit! I'm sick of it! I'm so done with this place. God, get me out of here now … *Now!*"

As he shouted, he hit the steering wheel repeatedly. He then sat back and took three deep breaths in and out. He said out loud to God in a soft manner, "God, I'm ready. I finally give my life to You. I'm done living it my way. I believe in You fully. Come into my heart, and be my Lord and Savior; I repent. If you've heard me, God, I thank You for Your grace. In Jesus's name, amen!"

He finally gave himself over to God. Cordell realized

that though he had avoided this earlier due to his discipline in staying away from that life of gangbanging, crime and violence and from the always-present Friday street party, he needed God because He was the only one who could fully protect him and bring him peace and a way out of this life. Cordell felt a weight lift from his shoulders. He started the car and drove home.

31

A couple of days after the altercation with Kenan, the Holy Spirit in Cordell prompted him to let go of the pain of murder through speaking and confessing to Ava. He didn't know how Ava would react. He was scared to tell her; he was terrified, in fact. As he sat in his car ready to take off and drive to Ava's, his heart was beating. He needed to phone her to tell her he was coming and that he had some things to talk about.

Ring-ring! "Hey, baby," answered Ava.

"Hey, baby. Is it OK if I come over?"

"Yeah, sure, I'm home now. You can come now if you want."

"OK, I'm coming over now, A. OK?"

"OK, see you in a little bit."

Pulling up outside Ava's house, he parked and sat there for an extra two minutes in order to catch his thoughts. Finally, he got out and rang the doorbell. Ava ran down the stairs, opened the door, and hugged Cordell all in one swift motion. "Hey, baby, you OK?" asked Ava with the brightest smile, exposing her deep dimples.

"Hey, baby, I'm OK. I just really need to talk to you. You're not gonna like it," replied Cordell, removing her arms from him while sighing at the same time. Her face changed;

it became an expression of worry. As they went to her room, Cordell was praying inside, *God, please put Your words in my mouth, and give her a heart of acceptance and forgiveness.*

They sat on her bed, and the conversation started. Cordell opened up about joining Big A's Piru gang. Then he opened up about Raymond's murder and how it was retribution for Big A's brother's death. Shortly thereafter, he opened up about Jayden's murder, Angel's murder, and Big A's murder. Ava was beside herself. She was in tears, speechless, shocked—not knowing what to do, she looked to the floor. "Ava, speak to me. What's going through your mind?"

Ava was silent, and when she looked up at him, all she could do was cry more. Cordell tried to grab her to draw her into his arms, but as he did, she stood up, quickly pulling away from him. At this point, the silence in the room was deafening. She looked at him with tears running down her face. After another couple of minutes of silence, Ava finally spoke. "Cordell, can you please go and sit on the stairs outside on the porch? I'll come and speak to you in a little bit."

"OK, baby," replied Cordell with worry.

Ava went to her knees and cried. After crying to herself, she started praying. "God, the God of Heaven, I've heard some things that are despicable. How can I be with a man as violent and wicked as this? What do I do now, God? What is the difference between him and Kenan, God? … God, I love Cordell, but how do I forget this?"

After she stayed still in silence waiting for a response, she heard from God in her spirit: *All these questions that you ask Me are questions you know the answer to, Ava. If a murderer can ask Me for forgiveness and salvation from their heart, and I can find it in My heart to forgive them and accept them, and if you are My representative, bearing My name, how can you not forgive Cordell?*

In that instance, Ava recognized that Cordell had given his life to Christ and that she had to overlook his transgressions. She was wise; she understood exactly what God was saying to her.

After another couple of minutes, she came out to the porch. Cordell turned around at the sound of the door with an eager face; he needed to know what she was thinking. As she looked at him, Cordell noticed that she had been weeping. Ava's eyes were red. She hugged him. To say this surprised him would be an understatement. The response so stunned Cordell that he couldn't even bring himself to hug her back; his arms were still by his sides.

Releasing him, Ava suggested that they both sit on the edge of the porch. "Cordell, I'm going to be honest here, OK? I didn't want to forgive you, and honestly, I didn't want to have anything to do with you … but God spoke to me after I told Him how I was feeling, and He said I have to forgive you, so Cordell, I forgive you." As Cordell was about to reply to that statement, Ava carried on while using her hand to gesture that he should just listen. "Just because I forgive you doesn't mean I should be with you or even be your friend, but … I came to the understanding that you gave your life to Christ not too long ago and you're a changed man. So I thought that now, as we are fully on the same page in terms of God, I am willing to still be here for you, but it will take me time to be normal with you."

In shock, Cordell began to cry. He could not believe that she forgave him for all the secrets and all the bad actions he performed. He was experiencing God's love and forgiveness again but through Ava this time. Cordell responded to her while wiping his eyes: "Thank you."

32

It had been one month since the encounter between Cordell and Kenan. Cordell didn't see Kenan around, and there was a different feel. Kenan had calmed down somehow, and there was a newfound peace in Cordell. As time had gone on, Kenan had come to the knowledge of Cordell's life-changing decision to dedicate himself to God. Kenan had lost this time. Cordell and Ava were preparing for college now, and Kenan couldn't bump into Cordell, as they were never in the same places anymore. Cordell had abandoned the Friday Crenshaw street party, and so had Ava.

On a random occasion one day, when Cordell was leaving with Ava to go off to college, Cordell saw Kenan hanging with his gang across the street. Cordell nodded at Kenan as a show of truce and respect. Kenan nodded back. Walking to the van he hired, Cordell held a big brown cardboard box. He was filling the back of the van with the stuff he packed for college. Finishing his packing, he closed the back door of the van and called his mum over, kissed her on the forehead, and hugged her tight.

Ava was in the passenger seat of the van, and as Cordell was about to open the driver's-side door, he stopped, looked around, and took a deep breath. He was thinking about all he had been through in this one year, but he said to himself,

If it wasn't for all of that, I may not have found God, and I would be dead by now. He looked down at his left forearm's full tattoo sleeve that he got when he joined the gang, and he had a small tear in his eye as he got to Jayden and Big A's faces and the statements he had gotten for both of them, which took up the whole inside of his forearm. He then wiped the tear and got into the van and said to Ava, "Are you ready for the next step in our journey?"

"Yeah, baby. I can't wait to get to college."

"Let's get out of here, then, baby."

Lightning Source UK Ltd.
Milton Keynes UK
UKHW010735051021
391704UK00002B/347

9 781728 387413